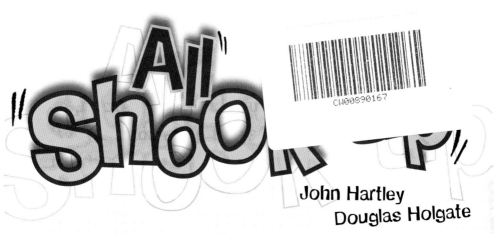

All "Shook Up"

John Hartley
Douglas Holgate

NELSON
CENGAGE Learning

Australia • Brazil • Japan • Korea • Mexico • Singapore • Spain • United Kingdom • United States

NELSON
CENGAGE Learning

All Shook Up

Text: John Hartley
Illustrations: Douglas Holgate
Editor: Rebecca Crisp
Design: Jennifer Warwick
Series design: James Lowe
Production controller: Lisa Porter
Reprint: Siew Han Ong

Fast Forward Independent Texts
Level 19

Text © 2009 Cengage Learning Australia Pty Limited
Illustrations © 2009 Cengage Learning Australia Pty Limited

Copyright Notice
This Work is copyright. No part of this Work may be reproduced, stored in a retrieval system, or transmitted in any form or by any means without prior written permission of the Publisher. Except as permitted under the Copyright Act 1968, for example any fair dealing for the purposes of private study, research, criticism or review, subject to certain limitations. These limitations include: Restricting the copying to a maximum of one chapter or 10% of this book, whichever is greater; Providing an appropriate notice and warning with the copies of the Work disseminated; Taking all reasonable steps to limit access to these copies to people authorised to receive these copies; Ensuring you hold the appropriate Licences issued by the Copyright Agency Limited ("CAL"), supply a remuneration notice to CAL and pay any required fees.

ISBN 978 0 17 017978 2
ISBN 978 0 17 017898 3 (set)

Cengage Learning Australia
Level 7, 80 Dorcas Street
South Melbourne, Victoria Australia 3205
Phone: 1300 790 853

Cengage Learning New Zealand
Unit 4B Rosedale Office Park
331 Rosedale Road, Albany, North Shore NZ 0632
Phone: 0508 635 766

For learning solutions, visit **cengage.com.au**

Printed in China by 1010 Printing International Ltd
2 3 4 5 6 7 15

All "Shook Up"

John Hartley
Douglas Holgate

Contents

CHAPTER 1

Just Another Day

It was Friday morning.
We were in class
doing some last-minute studying
for a science test.

"The test starts at 9.15," said Miss Evert.

Billy Buckley, late as usual,
walked in as Miss Evert was speaking.

"Can't do it, Miss," he said,
in a cheeky voice.
"I haven't got a pen."

Right at that second it started.
And I don't mean the test.

I noticed that the water
in the fish tank was moving
in tiny waves.
Then my pen started dancing
across my desk in little jumps.

I felt it
before I heard it.
Little vibrations started in my feet
and then travelled up my body.

Other kids had noticed too,
and Miss Evert had stopped writing
on the board.

There was a deep rumbling noise
coming from the ground.
It started quietly
but soon turned scary.
The whole classroom jumped
like a car going over a big bump
in the road.

Then there was quiet.

"Wow!" I said to Billy.
"That was an earthquake."

"Yeah," he whispered back.
His pale face looked as scared as I felt.

Rob Hart wasn't scared though.
He took our minds off our fear
by pretending he was Elvis Presley
strumming a guitar.

He wriggled his hips and sang,
"I'm all shook up, aha-ha ..."
Everyone laughed.

Is It Over?

Suddenly – bang!
The earthquake hit again,
harder and louder.

Windows rattled,
books fell from shelves,
and chairs fell over.

We were open-mouthed
and wide-eyed.
I had butterflies in my stomach
as big as eagles.

Suddenly Billy rushed for the door.

Miss Evert grabbed his arm to stop him.

"Stop! Don't go outside!" she shouted.

She turned to the rest of us.

"Everyone, get under your desks. Now!"

Bang!

The earthquake hit again.
The floor jumped and fell
like a ship on a rough sea.

As we dived under our desks,
a window broke.
More books and science equipment
fell to the floor.
Water sprayed from a broken tap.

Bang! Rumble! Boom!

The world went wild.

12

Forever

I don't know how long
the earthquake lasted,
but it seemed like forever.
Then after a while
the shocks grew smaller
and the rumbling got quieter.
Finally it was still.
We started to get up.

"Wait!" called Miss Evert.
"Wait another five minutes."

She was standing
in the doorway with Billy.
We waited under our desks.

"Just one more minute," called Miss Evert.

But as she spoke the shakes started again.

Bang! Bang! Bang!

The aftershocks rocked the building.
They were smaller than the first shakes
but still big enough to be scary.

Bang! Rumble! Boom!

The shakes and noises went on and on.

15

Finally the aftershocks stopped.
The classroom stopped shaking.

We got up and fixed up our chairs
and desks.

Still holding Billy's arm,
Miss Evert went around the room,
checking that no one was hurt.

"Just a little earthquake," she joked.
"Nothing to worry about!"

"I'm all shook up, aha-ha!" Rob sang again.

A Warm, Safe Blanket

Miss Evert leaned down
close to Billy's face.

"Are you alright?" she asked him quietly.
He nodded,
but he was very pale.

Then she sat down.

"Bring your chairs close," she said.
"I'll explain to you
about how earthquakes work
while we wait for your parents."

After the fear of the last few minutes
it was nice to sit
and listen to Miss Evert talk.
Nobody spoke.
Not even Billy, for a change.

Miss Evert's voice wrapped around us
like a warm, safe blanket.

Soon parents started arriving
to take their kids home.
They hugged their sons
and daughters tightly.
Many of them hugged Miss Evert too,
to say thanks for keeping their kids safe.

Mrs Buckley came to get Billy.
She cried even more than
all the other mums
when she heard about
what Miss Evert did.
She was very grateful to Miss Evert
for stopping Billy from running outside.

CHAPTER 5

A Change
for the Better

Dad came to get me.
We had to drive around fallen trees
and cracks in the ground to get home.

Lots of shop windows were broken,
and the lights weren't working.

The news said there was lots of damage
but that no one was badly injured.

22

Our house was fine, though.
A few windows were broken,
but that was the only damage.

The earthquake was really scary.
It shook us all up,
but I think it shook Billy up more.

On Monday, Billy was early to class.
He even brought a pen
and thanked Miss Evert
when she gave him his test paper.

Maybe it's good
to get "all shook up" sometimes,
but not too often!